Dear Parents,

Welcome to the Scholastic Reader series. We have taken over 80 years of experience with teachers, parents, and children and put it into a program that is designed to match your child's interests and skills.

Level 1—Short sentences and stories made up of words kids can sound out using their phonics skills and words that are important to remember.

Level 2—Longer sentences and stories with words kids need to know and new "big" words that they will want to know.

Level 3—From sentences to paragraphs to longer stories, these books have large "chunks" of texts and are made up of a rich vocabulary.

Level 4—First chapter books with more words and fewer pictures.

It is important that children learn to read well enough to succeed in school and beyond. Here are ideas for reading this book with your child:

- Look at the book together. Encourage your child to read the title and make a prediction about the story.
- Read the book together. Encourage your child to sound out words when appropriate. When your child struggles, you can help by providing the word.
- Encourage your child to retell the story. This is a great way to check for comprehension.
- Have your child take the fluency test on the last page to check progress.

Scholastic Readers are designed to support your child's efforts to learn how to read at every age and every stage. Enjoy helping your child learn to read and love to read.

—**Francie Alexander**
  Chief Education Officer
  Scholastic Education

To Michelle
— G.M.

The author and illustrator thank Manny Campana
for his contribution to this book.

Text copyright © 2004 by Grace Maccarone.
Illustrations copyright © 2004 by Norman Bridwell.
All rights reserved. Published by Scholastic Inc.
SCHOLASTIC, CARTWHEEL BOOKS, and associated logos
are trademarks and/or registered trademarks of Scholastic Inc.

Library of Congress Cataloging-in-Publication Data
Maccarone, Grace.
Magic Matt and the dinosaur/by Grace Maccarone; illustrated by Norman Bridwell.
    p. cm. — (Scholastic reader. Level 1) "Cartwheel Books."
Summary: After several attempts to conjure up a turtle, Magic Matt makes a dinosaur
appear, which seems like fun until he learns that a dinosaur is not the best pet.
Includes Matt's magic word and a list of other words that end in "le."
    ISBN 0-439-37607-6 (pbk. : alk. paper)
    [1. Magic—Fiction. 2. Dinosaurs—Fiction.] I. Bridwell, Norman, ill.
II. Title. III. Series.
PZ7.M1257 Mah 2004
[E]—dc21   2002152732
10 9 8 7 6 5 4 3 2 1   04 05 06 07 08
            Printed in the U.S.A. 23 • First printing, January 2004

by **Grace Maccarone**

Illustrated by **Norman Bridwell**

Scholastic Reader — Level 1

SCHOLASTIC INC.

New York   Toronto   London   Auckland   Sydney
Mexico City   New Delhi   Hong Kong   Buenos Aires

Hello! I am Magic Matt.
I can do magic.

See me make a turtle.
Zap!

No. That is a snake.
I want a turtle.
Zap!

No. That is a lizard.

I want a turtle.
Zap!

I made a dinosaur!
Cool!

Not so cool!
This dinosaur is a meat eater.

I will change it
to a plant eater.
Zap!

This is better.

Oh, no!
It eats our plants.
Mom will be mad.

Oh, no!
It breaks our chair.
Mom will be very,
very mad.

It runs out the door.
I run after it.

It chases a bus!

I must stop the dinosaur.
Zap!

Let's go home now, little turtle.

Magic Matt's Magic Words

"Turtle" ends in "le." Many other words also end in "le." Here are some of them:

apple
bubble
fiddle
giggle
little
needle
puddle
purple
table
title
wiggle

Fluency Fun

The words in each list below end in the same sounds.
Read the words in a list.
Read them again.
Read them faster.
Try to read all 12 words in one minute.

bake	bad	eat
cake	had	heat
make	mad	meat
take	sad	seat

Look for these words in the story.

no   **want**   **that**

our   **very**

Note to Parents:

According to *A Dictionary of Reading and Related Terms*, fluency is "the ability to read smoothly, easily, and readily with freedom from word-recognition problems." Fluency is necessary for good comprehension and enjoyable reading. The activities on this page include a speed drill and a sight-recognition drill. Speed drills build fluency because they help students rapidly recognize common syllables and spelling patterns in words, and they're fun! Sight-recognition drills help students smoothly and accurately recognize words. Practice these activities with your child to help him or her become a fluent reader.

—**Wiley Blevins**,
Reading Specialist